Mail for Husher Town

BY MARY LOUISE CUNEO

PICTURES BY PAM PAPARONE

Greenwillow Books · An Imprint of HarperCollinsPublishers

Husher Town is an animal town on the side of a mountain.

Four animals live there, in houses on Husher Street.

Bear, Cat, Donkey. And the monkey Ednabelle.

A girl has a house of her own on the mountaintop.

She looks down and sees things that happen in Husher Town. The girl is the animals' friend.

She has always lived on the mountain.

Her name is Julia.

One summer day Donkey finds an old leather sack.

"It's our mail sack," Ednabelle decides.

"And Bear is our mailman. He'll deliver the mail."

How? wonders Bear. How will Bear do that?

Cat whispers into her paws,

"Ooh, good! Husher Town mail!"

Donkey raises his head and brays, "VERY GOOD!
Husher Town mail!"

But day after day there is no mail.
That makes Cat, Donkey, and Ednabelle
mad at Bear.

Bear drags the empty sack up to the top of
the mountain.

"Everyone's mad at me because of no mail,"
he tells Julia.

"We have to think about this, Bear," Julia says.

Bear thinks, and goes to sleep on the top of
the mountain.

Julia thinks, and goes into her house.

After a while Bear hears Julia say,

"Bear, you'll be glad to wake up."

Julia is carrying a useful basket by its handle.

"In this basket," she says, "is Husher Town mail."

Julia takes the mail out of the basket.

She puts it down on the ground in two lines.

CAT

EDNABELLE

BEAR

DONKEY

The wide-awake Bear tiptoes up to the lines of mail.
One line is a line of fat envelopes.
A big name is written on each.
The other line is a line of boxes.
A big name is written on each.

"Every envelope has eight letters inside," Julia tells Bear. "The letters are Very Good papers—arithmetics and spellings—from school. The boxes have presents inside," Julia tells Bear. "Some time or other, there are boxes like these in everyone's mail."

Bear hugs his sack, then collects the mail. Boxes in his sack first. Envelopes on top of the boxes. "Julia," he says, "I can't sleep here on the top of the mountain any more now. I have to deliver the mail."

"I'll come and help," says Julia.

When the two of them step onto Husher Street, Bear
calls out, "Here's mail! Julia found the Husher Town mail!"
Cat purrs for the mail.
Donkey waves his ears for the mail.
Ednabelle orders, "Kindly deliver the mail!"
Bear delivers the envelopes. Julia helps by
reading names on envelopes. At each delivery
Bear is happy to say, "There are a lot of letters inside."

The animals open their envelopes and take out their letters.
Cat fluffs her letters with her tail.
"Is this what I do with my letters?" she asks.

Donkey walks onto his letters.
"Is this what I do with my letters?"
he asks.

Bear puts his head into the sack.

"What do we do with our letters?" he asks.

"What do we do!" Ednabelle scolds.

"Why, we hang our letters in a tree, of course!"

Bear brings his head out of the sack.

"Could we wait to hang our letters," he asks,

"until we open our boxes?"

"Boxes! What boxes? What's in the boxes?"

Cat, Donkey, and Ednabelle ask all at once.

Bear delivers the boxes.
Julia helps by reading names on boxes.
At each delivery Bear is happy to say,
"There are presents inside."

Cat's present is a tambourine.

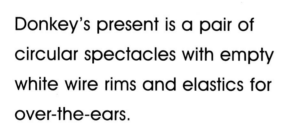

Donkey's present is a pair of
circular spectacles with empty
white wire rims and elastics for
over-the-ears.

Ednabelle's present is
a silver-colored whistle
on a long yellow ribbon.

Bear's present is a baseball cap.

Julia whispers to Bear, "The letters on the cap are C-U-B-S. That spells 'cubs,' Bear."

Bear whispers back, "Julia, that's what I was. I was a cubs with my sisters and brothers. And," he adds, "with a number of others."

The animals thank Julia for finding the mail.

Bear remembers a song to sing: "For she's a jolly good Julia!"

Cat, Donkey, and Ednabelle clap with the singing.

It's time to hang the letters.

Bear hangs letters on low branches. He wears his present on the top of his head.

Donkey puts on his present and watches. "What a good job!" he exclaims to Cat. "And look at Ednabelle high in the air!"

"I can't look," murmurs Cat, covering her face with her present.

When the thirty-two letters are hung, Ednabelle says, "It's perfect mail. It flutters just right. We'll have a parade now, around the letter tree."

Ednabelle gives instructions to Cat, Donkey, and Bear about how to parade.

Julia hurries up to the top of the mountain for the best possible view of the Husher Town parade.

She sees Ednabelle leading the parade, whistling her whistle. She sees Cat next, with her tambourine in her mouth. Cat is nodding her head, mixing tambourine jingles into Ednabelle's whistlings.

Donkey is third, looking wise in his spectacles, like an important person who'll soon make a speech. Julia sees Bear at the end of the parade. Bear smiles as he marches around and around. Again and again he raises his CUBS cap and waves to the letters.

Julia sees that the letters wave back.

The first time, Julia thinks, that letters have ever waved back to their mailman.

THE END

This book is for the champion Cubs fan in the family—
my husband, Paul Cuneo —M. L. C.

For Richard —P. P.

Acrylics were used for the full-color art. The text type is Avant Garde.

Mail for Husher Town. Text copyright © 2000 by Mary Louise Cuneo. Illustrations copyright © 2000 by Pam Paparone.
Printed in Singapore by Tien Wah Press. All rights reserved. http://www.harperchildrens.com

Library of Congress Cataloging-in-Publication Data
Cuneo, Mary Louise. Mail for Husher Town / by Mary Louise Cuneo; pictures by Pam Paparone.   p.   cm.
"Greenwillow Books."   Summary: With Julia's help, Bear delivers the mail to the other toy animals in her room, Cat,
Donkey, and Ednabelle the monkey.   ISBN 0-688-16525-7.   [1. Letter carriers—Fiction.   2. Animals—Fiction.
3. Toys—Fiction.   4. Play—Fiction.]   I. Paparone, Pamela, ill.   II. Title.   PZ7.C91615Mai   2000
[E]—dc21   98-52877   CIP   AC

1 2 3 4 5 6 7 8 9 10 First Edition